HIGHS
LOWS!!

AMAR SINGH

BlueRose ONE
Stories Matter
NewDelhi • London

BLUEROSE PUBLISHERS
India | U.K.

Copyright © Amar Singh 2025

All rights reserved by author. No part of this publication may be reproduced, stored in a retrieval system or transmitted in any form or by any means, electronic, mechanical, photocopying, recording or otherwise, without the prior permission of the author. Although every precaution has been taken to verify the accuracy of the information contained herein, the publisher assumes no responsibility for any errors or omissions. No liability is assumed for damages that may result from the use of information contained within.

BlueRose Publishers takes no responsibility for any damages, losses, or liabilities that may arise from the use or misuse of the information, products, or services provided in this publication.

For permissions requests or inquiries regarding this publication,
please contact:
BLUEROSE PUBLISHERS
www.BlueRoseONE.com
info@bluerosepublishers.com
+91 8882 898 898
+4407342408967

ISBN: 978-93-6452-448-3

Typesetting: Sagar

First Edition: January 2025

Disclaimer

The content in this book is purely a work of fiction. All the names, places, and characters mentioned in the book are fictional creations of the author. Some parts of the story are influenced by real incidents, which have been re-created using fictional names, places, and characters. Any resemblance to actual events, locales, or persons, living or dead, is entirely coincidental. The views and opinions expressed in this book are those of the author and do not necessarily reflect the official policy or position of any other individual, organization, employer, or company.

This book is not intended as a substitute for professional advice. Readers should consult appropriate professionals regarding their individual circumstances.

Preface

Life is a tapestry of trials and triumphs, each thread a story of resilience and transformation. This book chronicles the remarkable journey of a boy whose life was marked by profound upheavals and unexpected turns. It is a tale of betrayal, adversity, and ultimate redemption that I believe will resonate deeply with readers.

The story begins with a chance encounter between our protagonist, Ravi, and an old schoolmate, Richa. This reunion, filled with joy and nostalgia, quickly takes an unexpected turn during an unplanned visit to Richa's home. The awkward circumstances that arise force Ravi to confront a tumultuous past, setting off a chain of events that test his spirit and fortitude. During this visit, Dev, Richa's husband, humiliates Ravi because of his past. Richa, unaware of the history between Ravi and Dev, attempts to calm the situation but Ravi, overwhelmed, flees. Through Richa's persistent efforts, she eventually convinces Ravi to share his college story, unfolding the narrative that defines this book.

Ravi's story is one of intense struggles. Betrayed by a close friend, he was expelled from college. One of his dearest friends faced dire consequences, and even his father refused to allow him to come back home. These events left Ravi marred by circumstances, prompting his move to Chennai in search of a fresh start. Yet, his challenges were far from over. In Chennai, Ravi struggled to find his footing, grappling with the weight of his past and the uncertainties of his future. His journey then took him to Delhi, where he met a noble and compassionate figure—the Chairperson of a renowned coaching institute. This pivotal meeting became a beacon of hope, offering not just employment but a renewed sense of purpose and direction. The mentorship and kindness he received sparked a dramatic turnaround, transforming his life in ways he had never imagined.

This book is more than just the story of one boy's struggles and victories. It is a testament to the human capacity for resilience, the power of kindness, and the profound impact of second chances. It highlights how, even in our darkest hours, we can find light and support in the most unexpected places. Writing this story has been an emotional journey, a reminder of the indomitable spirit that resides within us all. It has reinforced my belief in the goodness of people and the possibility of redemption, no matter how far one has fallen.

I am deeply grateful to those who shared their insights and experiences, providing a richer context for this narrative. Their contributions have been instrumental in bringing this story to life. To my family and friends, your support has been unwavering, and for that, I am eternally thankful.

As you delve into the pages of this book, I hope you will find inspiration in Ravi's journey. May it encourage you to believe in the power of perseverance, the importance of empathy, and the possibility of change. This is a story for anyone who has faced adversity and dreamed of a brighter tomorrow.

Thank you for joining me on this journey. May it offer you hope, insight, and a renewed belief in the power of the human spirit.

With gratitude,

Amar Singh

Acknowledgement

First and foremost, I extend my deepest gratitude to God for inspiring me with the thoughts and reflections that shaped this book. This journey would not have been possible without divine guidance.

My heartfelt thanks go to my students, whose constant motivation and encouragement ignited the spark of writing within me. Their unwavering support has been the driving force behind every page of this book. They have shown me the profound impact a teacher-student relationship can have, and for that, I am eternally grateful.

Special thanks to Shruti, who took on the crucial task of finalising the illustrations in this book. Her dedication and eye for detail have brought the story to life in a way that words alone could not achieve.

I am profoundly grateful to Samarth, Ananya, and Jia for generously dedicating their time and effort to the meticulous editing of the content. Their expertise and patience have been invaluable, ensuring the narrative flows seamlessly.

To all my students from every place I have taught, I express my sincere appreciation. Their belief in me as a teacher has been transformative, and this book stands as a testament to what can be achieved through mutual respect and inspiration.

I owe a great deal of gratitude to my wife and my son for their patience, understanding, and unwavering support throughout this journey. Their love and encouragement have been my pillars of strength.

Lastly, I extend my thanks to all my family members, friends, and well-wishers. Their support and encouragement have been instrumental in bringing this book to fruition.

And to you, the reader, thank you for choosing this book. I hope it brings you as much insight and inspiration as it brought me in writing it.

With gratitude,

Amar Singh

Contents

1. A Chanced Encounter 1
2. An Unexpected Reunion: Shadows of The Past 6
3. Echoes of Regret Revisiting the Past 11
4. Dormitory Debates and Dining Hall Delights: Navigating College Life 15
5. Homeward Bound: Trials and Triumphs of the Return 24
6. Cheers to Chaos: Navigating Exam Season 29
6. From Books to Banquets: Celebrating Krishav's Success 34
7. Cracking the Code: The Mystery of Krishav's Success 39
8. Dorm Drift: Friendship Fluctuations 43
9. Glamour and Envy: Krishav's Birthday Bash 46
10. Golden Bonds: Friendship and Ambition 50
11. Dorm Drama: Betrayal and Blowback 54
12. Paths to Reconciliation 57
13. Love: Life-time Pain 61
14. Broken Trust: The Cost of Ignoring Warning Signs 66
15. Pari's Plight 72
16. End of College Life 75
17. Chennai Episode 79
18. Delhi Episode 84
19. The Turning Point 89
20. Realisation, Regret, and Gratitude 93

1. A Chanced Encounter

When I finally managed to board the train, I was completely out of breath. The hustle of making it just in time, after realising that my decision to take the train instead of a flight was a mistake, left me exhausted. The flight, though heavy on my pocket, would have spared me this chaos. Anyway, as I reached my berth, I noticed it was already occupied by a smartly dressed, tall, and beautiful woman, likely in her mid-thirties.

The dim lighting of the train compartment cast a soft glow on her, highlighting her elegant features. Her long, dark hair fell in waves around her shoulders, and her eyes sparkled with a mix of surprise and recognition. As we exchanged glances, she spoke up, her voice melodious and familiar, "I'm getting off at the next station." She had a very young girl sleeping next to her, comfortably nestled on my berth. Out of courtesy, I gestured that she could sit there, and I settled at the corner.

Ever since our eyes met, I had a nagging feeling that I had seen her somewhere before, or that she was someone quite significant to me. However, I couldn't recall where we had met. She, too, seemed to steal a glance at me once or twice. Before I could muster the courage to say anything, she exclaimed, "Is that you, Ravi from Bal Bharti... 2003 batch?"

My mouth dropped open in astonishment, and then a broad smile spread across my face. "Richa...! The all-time beauty." She had been pretty ever since I had known her, which was back in the 4th standard. Meeting her after all these years was the best coincidence that had happened to me in a long time.

She looked even more beautiful than before, with a glow that seemed to emanate from within. Her elegance and the ease with which she carried herself were mesmerising. All the past memories seemed to have been refreshed. As we reminisced about our school days, the years melted away, and it felt as though no time had passed since we last saw each other.

We began talking about our old school days, our friends, and the mischievous pranks we used to play. The train's rhythmic clatter provided a nostalgic soundtrack to our conversation, making the moment even more surreal. Richa's laughter was infectious, and her eyes sparkled with joy as she recounted stories of our childhood.

As the train rattled on, we lost ourselves in conversation, catching up on lost time and reliving cherished memories. It was a serendipitous encounter that reminded me of the beauty of unexpected connections and the power of nostalgia. She told me about her husband, who was a software engineer at a renowned IT company in Gurgaon, Haryana, and the boutique she ran in Noida.

Her description of her boutique was vivid. She painted a picture of a cosy, elegant space filled with vibrant fabrics, intricate designs, and a welcoming atmosphere. I could almost see her there, guiding customers through the racks, her eyes alight with passion for her craft.

Richa shared stories of her life since our school days, and I marvelled at how much she had accomplished. Besides managing her boutique, she had pursued her passion for art and was now a renowned painter, travelling the world to showcase her work. Her eyes lit up as she talked about her exhibitions in Paris, New York, and Tokyo, and I could sense the deep satisfaction she derived from her work.

Witnessing her achievements and glories, I couldn't reveal my plight. I went on to boast about my fake achievements and cooked up a story of whatever I could think of. Later,

I felt as if I had exaggerated a bit too much. Nevertheless, my sole focus was to cast an impression on her at that time. I told her about my adventures, my career in teaching, and the ups and downs I had faced along the way. She listened intently, her eyes never leaving mine, making me feel as though my stories were the most important thing in the world to her at that moment.

I was surprised to learn that she still remembered my so-called "relationship" that I had confided in her when we first met back in 1999. She asked me, half teasingly, where my crush was. I replied in the same light-hearted manner, telling her that she was settled with her husband in Kisumu, where he worked as a veterinary physician in Nairobi. Richa showed her curated sympathy, and we both giggled, letting the moment pass with shared laughter.

As the conversation flowed, I found myself drawn to her in a way I hadn't anticipated. There was a warmth in her presence, a familiarity that felt like coming home. I wondered if she felt the same, or if I was just being overly nostalgic for no significant reason. The train's gentle rocking seemed to lull the rest of the world into the background, making our little corner feel like a universe unto itself.

Richa was telling me about her family when I cut her short, surprising even myself with my boldness. "Richa, there's something I've never told anyone," I began, my voice suddenly serious. She looked at me, curiosity and concern mingling in her eyes.

"I've always wondered what might have been if we had stayed in touch," I confessed, my heart pounding in my chest. "I always felt there was something special between us, even back then."

Richa's eyes widened slightly, and for a moment, she was silent. The train's rhythmic clatter seemed to amplify the tension in the air. Then, she smiled a soft, wistful smile that made my heart ache.

"Ravi," she said gently, "I've thought about you too, more often than I care to admit. But life took us in different directions, and we both found our own paths."

Her words were extremely soothing to me, yet they also stirred a longing that I had buried long ago. The truth was out, and there was no taking it back. The air between us crackled with unspoken emotions, a mixture of relief, regret, and a glimmer of hope.

******

2. An Unexpected Reunion: Shadows of The Past

As the night deepened, we continued talking, our voices low and intimate in the quiet of the sleeping train. The young girl next to Richa stirred but didn't wake, her peaceful slumber a stark contrast to the whirlwind of emotions between us.

Richa told me more about her life, her travels, and her art. She showed me pictures of her paintings on her phone, each one a testament to her talent and passion. I was captivated not just by her art, but by the way her eyes sparkled when she talked about it, the way her whole being seemed to light up with joy.

In return, I shared my own stories, my successes and failures, my dreams and fears. It felt good to open up, to share parts of myself that I hadn't shared with anyone in years. There was something about Richa that made it easy—to be honest, to be vulnerable.

As the first light of dawn began to filter through the train's windows, casting a soft glow over everything, I felt a sense of urgency. Our time together was running out. Richa's stop was approaching, and soon she would be gone, perhaps forever.

"Richa," I said, my voice trembling slightly, "I don't want to lose you again. I know it's crazy, but would you consider staying in touch? Maybe we could... see where things go?"

She looked at me, her eyes searching mine. For a moment, I feared she would say no, that she would walk away and leave me with nothing but memories. But then, she smiled, a smile that reached her eyes and warmed my heart.

"I'd like that, Ravi," she said softly. "I'd like that very much."

As the train slowed to a stop at her destination, we both stood up, the weight of our conversation hanging in the air. She gently woke the young girl, who blinked sleepily and clung to her mother's hand. I helped Richa gather her bags, and we walked to the door together.

Standing there, on the platform, we shared a moment of quiet understanding. The train's whistle blew, signalling its imminent departure. We exchanged phone numbers and promised to stay in touch.

"Take care, Richa," I said, my voice thick with emotion. "You too, Ravi," she replied, her eyes glistening with unshed tears.

And then she was gone, walking away with the young girl in tow, disappearing into the crowd. I watched until she was out of sight, a sense of loss mingling with a newfound hope.

As the train pulled away from the station, I settled back into my berth, a smile playing on my lips. The encounter with Richa had been unexpected, but it had rekindled something in me that I thought was long lost. The past had a way of catching up with us, but sometimes, it brought with it the promise of a new beginning.

Richa and I stayed in touch, true to our promise. Our conversations over the phone were filled with laughter, shared memories, and the tentative exploration of a future together. The spark that had been reignited on that train ride grew stronger with each passing day.

Months later, I found myself standing in front of her boutique in Noida, my heart pounding with anticipation. As the door opened and I saw Richa's smiling face, I knew that our unexpected reunion had been the start of something beautiful. I seemed to have been given a second chance, and this time, I was determined to make the most of it.

I handed her the bouquet that I had brought especially for her. She told me that she was about to leave for her home as it was her husband's birthday that day. To my dismay, I thought I wouldn't be able to spend time with her. I told her to convey my best wishes to her husband and turned to move back. However, she insisted that I join them for the party at home. Initially, I said no, but my longing to spend time with her won over me and I assented to her proposal of attending her husband's birthday party.

She drove me to her home, located in the upscale neighbourhood of South Delhi. Her daughter, barely five years old, took on the role of grandmother of the house, directing Rekha Didi and Uday Bhaiya, the household staff, with surprising authority. Her demeanour seemed far too mature for her tender age as she orchestrated the placement of objects with precision.

Meanwhile, her husband, a strikingly tall and handsome man, entered the room, a faint gleam accentuating his well-groomed beard. As I extended my hand and raised my gaze to meet his, a jolt of recognition shot through me—he was my college batchmate. Inwardly, I cursed the cruel twist of destiny that brought us together. Why now, of all times?

Fortunately, it seemed he hadn't recognized me at first glance. I averted my gaze, hoping to maintain the facade of anonymity.

Richa introduced me to Dev, saying, "Dev, meet my school friend Ravi. Remember, I told you about him? We met on the train, and he graciously offered me a seat at his place." As Richa spoke, I sensed Dev's fixed stare on me, and I knew the moment of anonymity was fleeting.

"Ravi... ISS... 2005 batch, Mechanical... college drop-out... right?!" His words dripped with mockery, and I felt a pang of humiliation.

"Oh! So now, you've become a Master Ji... Ha... Ha... ha... and teaching English, is it? That's quite the transformation for this HINDI MEDIUM GUY... eh?"

Even Richa seemed taken aback by Dev's sudden change in tone. "Ravi... What's going on...? You're an engineer!"

She shot a pleading glance at Dev, silently urging him to cease his verbal assault. It was clear she was uncomfortable with the direction the conversation had taken.

Not wanting to mar their gathering any further, I made a hasty exit, murmuring, "Richa…, I'll catch up with you later." But as I walked away, the echoes of Dev's taunts— "loser… college drop-out… Hindi-medium…"— resounded in my ears, a relentless reminder of my tarnished past.

Feeling utterly defeated, I berated myself all the way home. I couldn't shake off the regret of ever meeting Richa on that train, or of visiting her boutique. The weight of disappointment hung heavy on my shoulders, casting a shadow over every step.

******

3. Echoes of Regret
Revisiting the Past

Days turned into weeks, and the sting of that humiliating encounter lingered. I avoided Richa's calls and messages, too ashamed to face her. She tried reaching out several times, her concern evident in her words, but I couldn't bring myself to respond. The weight of my lies and the harsh reality of my past made it impossible to confront her.

Life continued its monotonous rhythm, and I buried myself in work. Teaching English to students who reminded me of my younger self, full of dreams and aspirations, became my solace. I poured all my energy into helping them succeed, determined to give them the chances I had squandered.

One evening, as I was grading papers in my modest apartment, my phone buzzed with a message. It was from Richa. "Ravi, I know you're avoiding me, but we need to talk. Please meet me at the cafeteria near our old school this Saturday. It's important."

Curiosity and a sense of duty compelled me to go. We could easily see the buildings of our old school from this cafeteria. Our old school, Bal Bharti, held so many memories. The sight of the familiar building brought a wave of nostalgia, mingled with a sense of dread. I walked through the gates and headed to the playground where we used to spend our recess.

Richa was waiting for me, looking as elegant as ever. The moment she saw me, she smiled, but there was sadness in her eyes. "Ravi, thank you for coming."

"I didn't have much of a choice," I replied, trying to keep my tone light but failing miserably.

She took a deep breath. "Ravi, I want to apologise for what happened that day. Dev's behaviour was unacceptable, and I had no idea about your past. I'm sorry you had to go through that."

"It's not your fault, Richa. I should have been honest with you from the start," I admitted, the words feeling like a weight lifted off my chest.

She nodded. "We've all made mistakes, Ravi. But that doesn't define who we are now. I still remember the kind, talented boy from school who had big dreams. I see that same person in you today."

Her words touched me deeply, and for the first time in weeks, I felt a sense of hope. "Thank you, Richa. That means a lot."

Richa's question pierced through the veil of my composure, stirring up a storm of emotions that I had long suppressed. Her genuine concern and curiosity touched a tender spot in my heart, urging me to peel back the layers of my past and reveal the raw, unfiltered truth.

As I met Richa's gaze, my mind drifted back to a time when dreams seemed within reach, when the sky was not just a canvas of endless blue but a boundless realm of possibilities. "You see, Richa," I began, my voice tinged with a mixture of nostalgia and regret, "life has a way of leading us down unexpected paths, even when we have our hearts set on something else."

With a heavy sigh, I delved into the depths of my memories, retracing the footsteps of my younger self, brimming with ambition and fuelled by a fervent desire to soar amongst the clouds as a pilot. "Flying was more than just a dream for me," I confessed, my eyes shimmering with the echoes of lost aspirations. "It was a passion that ignited my soul, a calling that whispered promises of adventure and freedom."

Taking a deep breath, I began to unravel the tangled threads of my past. "It's actually a long story, you see," I began, a distant look in my eyes as I recalled the past. "After 10th standard, you shifted to Noida and my life took a different turn. I joined an all-boys school for my intermediate studies, which was a significant change from the co-ed environment we were used to. The atmosphere was intense, competitive, and rigorous, pushing me to new limits. I dedicated myself to my studies, driven by the desire to succeed and make something of myself. The amity among the boys was strong, and the friendships I forged there became an important part of my journey. The rigorous academic environment, combined with the supportive yet challenging peer group, laid a strong foundation for my future endeavours.

As the months turned into years, my efforts began to pay off. I managed to score impressively well in my

Engineering Entrance Exam, a result of countless sleepless nights and relentless hard work. The competition was fierce, but my determination never wavered. I remember the anxiety and excitement that gripped me as I waited for the results, hoping that my dreams would become a reality. When the results were finally announced, I felt a rush of relief and joy; I had secured a high score, enough to get me admitted to the Indian School of Science (ISS-Name Changed), one of the most prestigious Engineering institutions in the country. The sense of accomplishment was overwhelming, knowing that all my hard work had paid off and I was on the path to achieving my goals.

To my fortune, not only did I gain admission to ISS, but I also got my preferred stream of study. This was a dream come true for me, as I had always been passionate about this particular field. The prospect of studying at such a renowned institution, surrounded by some of the brightest minds, filled me with both excitement and apprehension. I knew that the road ahead would be challenging, but I was ready to embrace it with open arms. My time at ISS was transformative, as it provided me with invaluable knowledge, skills, and experiences that would shape my future. It was here that I began to see the broader picture of my aspirations and started laying the groundwork for my career.

******

4. Dormitory Debates and Dining Hall Delights: Navigating College Life

The first few months of college life felt like a dream come true. The sprawling campus seemed to beckon with promise, and I found myself immersed in a world of endless possibilities. Among the three boys' hostels, Radhakrishnan Hostel, the third and reputedly the best, became my home away from home. The hostel life was a vibrant tapestry of friendship and laughter, with each day bringing new adventures and discoveries.

HIGHS LOWS

In Radhakrishnan Hostel, I found myself surrounded by colourful characters, each adding their own unique flavour to the mix. My roommates, Vengadesh from Gopalganj, Bihar, and Avaneesh from Chitrakoot, Uttar Pradesh, couldn't have been more different. Vengadesh, with his larger-than-life persona, never missed an opportunity to regale us with tales of his supposed riches and influence back home. His exaggerated claims often led to spirited debates, with us teasing him mercilessly about his obsession with Gopalganj. No matter the topic, Vengadesh always had a way of turning the conversation back to his beloved hometown.

Vengadesh: Hey, you know, in Gopalganj, we have everything you can imagine. Riches, influence, you name it, we've got it.

Me: (chuckling) Oh, really? So, if I said there's a McDonald's in Gopalganj, you'd probably tell me they're planning to open a branch on every street corner, right?

Vengadesh: (nodding enthusiastically) Exactly! In fact, they're already scouting locations for the next one as we speak.

Me: (laughing) Wow, Gopalganj sounds like the place to be!

Avaneesh: (interjecting with a grin) Yeah, and I heard they're planning to build a Taj Mahal replica next to the local chai shop.

Vengadesh: (nodding seriously) Oh, absolutely. It's going to be the eighth wonder of the world, mark my words.

Me: (laughing) Well, I'll be sure to visit Gopalganj soon then. Who knows, maybe I'll catch a glimpse of the Gopalganj version of the Eiffel Tower while I'm at it!

On the other hand, Avaneesh was the quiet anchor amidst our lively banter. With a subtle smile and a twinkle in his eye, he would observe our antics with quiet amusement, rarely interjecting except to offer a witty remark or a well-timed joke. Despite his reserved nature, Avaneesh had a way of effortlessly endearing himself to us, his silent presence adding a touch of serenity to our otherwise chaotic dorm room. Together, the three of us formed an unlikely trio, each bringing our own quirks and personalities to the table, bound together by the shared experience of navigating the exhilarating highs and inevitable lows of college life.

Despite the academic divide between Vengadesh, Avaneesh, and me—Vengadesh and Avaneesh from Computer Science, and myself pursuing Mechanical Engineering—we found a common ground in room number 13, Rahul's haven. Rahul, hailing from Auraiya, Uttar Pradesh, now a distinguished Bank Manager in an international institution at Tybee Island, Georgia, graciously opened his doors to us, creating a sanctuary for solidarity and shared learning.

Raj, a fellow student from Aryabhatta hostel, became a familiar face in Rahul's room, often joining us for study sessions and collaborative learning. Coming from an English Medium background, Raj brought a fresh perspective to our discussions and studies. His knack for simplifying complex concepts and his willingness to lend a helping hand made him an invaluable asset in our academic pursuits.

Together, in the cosy confines of Rahul's room, we formed a makeshift study group, united by our shared passion for learning and our determination to excel in our respective fields. Whether it was grappling with the intricacies of Mechanical Engineering or delving into the nuances of computer science, we leaned on each other for support and guidance, forging bonds that would withstand the test of time and distance.

Our Professional Communication (PC) classes, led by the charismatic CP Johnson Thomas Sir, were the undisputed highlight of our week, eagerly anticipated despite their bi-weekly occurrence. Sir's presence brought an air of excitement and anticipation, infusing each session with his easy-going demeanour and infectious energy. With a penchant for cracking jokes and even breaking into dance on occasion, Sir's classes were nothing short of a breath of fresh air, providing much-needed relief from the rigours of academic life.

In Sir's classroom, laughter flowed freely, and the atmosphere was always filled with positivity and warmth. His ability to effortlessly blend humour with valuable lessons in communication made every session both enjoyable and enlightening. Whether he was sharing anecdotes from his own experiences or imparting practical tips for effective communication, Sir had a way of engaging his students and leaving a lasting impression.

But perhaps the most remarkable aspect of Sir's classes was their transformative effect on us. Each session served as a veritable stress-buster, offering a brief respite from the pressures of exams and assignments. By the time we left the classroom, we felt refreshed and uplifted, armed with newfound confidence and ready to tackle whatever challenges lay ahead. Sir's classes were more than just lessons in communication—they were moments of inspiration and empowerment that left a lasting impact on all who attended.

And then, there was the culinary delight that was Mr. Reddy's Mess. With its tantalising array of South Indian delicacies—sambhars, rasams, idlis, and more—it was a gastronomic adventure for us North Indians, albeit one that required some adjustment. Yet, amidst the initial struggles to adapt to the new flavours and textures, there was a certain charm to the communal dining experience, where friendships were forged over shared meals and culinary discoveries.

But amidst the comradeship and culinary delights, our academic journey hit a roadblock with the introduction of two formidable subjects: Thermodynamics and Engineering Drawing. And to add to the challenge, Krishav, the enigmatic son of a local politician, entered our midst. Endowed with lavish comforts and material possessions, Krishav's ostentatious displays of wealth were the stuff of envy and curiosity.

Whenever we spotted Krishav on campus, he was always the centre of attention, throwing lavish parties and flaunting his wealth. His disregard for studies made it crystal clear that academics were the least of his priorities. So, it was only natural for us to believe that his admission to ISS was a direct result of his father's towering influence and social standing. It seemed like yet another instance where connections and privilege opened doors that hard work and merit alone couldn't. But to our astonishment, the reality was far more intricate. Beneath the surface of what appeared to be a typical case of nepotism, there was an unexpected twist—something we hadn't even considered, something that turned our assumptions completely upside down.

As we delved deeper into our studies and navigated the complex web of social dynamics within our college community, our once seamless academic journey began to unravel, presenting us with challenges that tested our resilience and unity in ways we had never imagined. With each passing day, we uncovered new layers to Krishav's persona, each revelation painting a picture of a lifestyle that seemed worlds apart from our own.

We discovered that Krishav had a penchant for indulgence, his room window serving as a clandestine gateway to a world of vices. From cigarettes to other illicit substances, he spared no expense in satisfying his desires, often enlisting the help of Vishwa, the warden's attendant, to procure these forbidden goods. It was a revelation that left us both intrigued and disheartened, as the allure of Krishav's extravagant lifestyle tempted us, even as we grappled with our moral compasses.

Despite our curiosity and the pull towards his lavish existence, Krishav's haughty and arrogant demeanour served as a barrier, preventing us from forming any meaningful connections with him. While we were drawn to the allure of his lifestyle, his attitude alienated us, leaving us on the sidelines, mere spectators to his opulent world. And so, we found ourselves torn between the desire for companionship and the reluctance to associate with someone whose values clashed so starkly with our own.

As we observed Krishav from a distance, we couldn't help but wonder what lay beneath the facade of wealth and privilege. Not knowing that our paths would soon intertwine in ways that would challenge our perceptions and redefine the boundaries of friendship and loyalty.

On Fresher's Day, I found myself in a desperate situation—I needed a pair of green shoes to adhere to the dress code, but buying them for just one occasion felt like an extravagance I couldn't afford. Asking my dad for money was out of the question. That's when Rahul came to my rescue, suggesting I borrow a pair from Krishav, who happened to have a spare. Reluctantly, I agreed, though the thought of borrowing made me uneasy.

To my surprise, Krishav readily agreed to lend me his shoes, even offering his tie to complete my outfit. It was a small act of kindness, but it meant the world to me, marking the beginning of an unexpected friendship. I wondered if this simple gesture would set the stage for a series of events that would change everything.

Later that day, as we celebrated, Krishav offered us a drink. A sense of unease washed over both Rahul and me, a gut feeling that something wasn't right. But under the weight of obligation—the borrowed tie and shoes—we felt powerless to refuse. It was a moment tinged with uncertainty and apprehension, foreshadowing the twists and turns our newfound friendship would take in the days to come.

After the excitement of Fresher's Week faded, we were granted a short but much-needed seven-day pre-semester break. As expected, Krishav already had a jam-packed itinerary, brimming with parties, road trips, and extravagant plans. To our surprise, he wanted us to be a part of his adventure-packed holiday. But after weeks of being swept up in his non-stop show of wealth and energy, we felt the need to hit the pause button and take a step back. Personally, I was craving a break from it all, a chance to breathe. Homesickness hit me hard, and the looming festival season only made it worse. Diwali was just around the corner—three days away. The thought of missing out on the vibrant lights, the echo of laughter with family, the warmth of home-cooked meals, and the joy of lighting diyas with loved ones was too much to bear. So, I made my decision: I packed my bags and set off for home, eager to leave behind the glitz and chaos of campus life and immerse myself in the comforting embrace of my city, my home, and my people.

******

5. Homeward Bound: Trials and Triumphs of the Return

I couldn't contain my excitement as the day approached for my journey back home. It had been nearly five long months since I left the comfort of my home. Eager to reunite with my family, I made arrangements to book my train tickets.

Unfortunately, my plans hit a snag when the student I had asked to book my tickets messed up with me. Left without a reserved seat on the train, I faced the prospect of an expensive and tiresome journey home. With no other choice, I embarked on a long and arduous journey, travelling first by bus from Indore to Kanpur, and then by train from Kanpur to Prayagraj.

The bus journey from Indore was relatively smooth sailing, thanks to the comfort of a sleeper bus. I settled in and managed to catch some much-needed rest as the miles passed by beneath me. However, the next leg of my journey, from Kanpur in a local train's general compartment, proved to be a different story altogether. As I found myself squeezed into the overcrowded compartment, I couldn't help but feel a sense of discomfort creeping in. To make matters worse, two elderly gentlemen nearby were engrossed in a spirited debate, their voices raised above the din of the train. What caught my attention, however, was the familiar sound of chewing pan, their mouths stained red from the betel leaf they were chewing. As they argued, flecks of the betel leaf and nuts flew in all directions, including onto me and the other passengers nearby.

It was a frustrating and unpleasant experience, to say the least. But amidst the chaos and discomfort, I couldn't help but find a hint of irony in the situation—a reminder that sometimes, the journey home isn't always smooth sailing, but it's the destination that makes it all worthwhile.

Finally, I was back home, surrounded by the familiar sights and sounds of my city. The air was filled with the comforting aroma of home-cooked meals, and the streets bustled with the hustle and bustle of everyday life. As I reunited with my family and friends, a sense of nostalgia washed over me, enveloping me in a warm embrace. It was a feeling like no other—being back among my people, in the place where I belonged. Every corner of the city held a memory, every face a story. It was as if time stood still, allowing me to savour each moment and treasure the bonds that tied me to this place. Amidst the laughter and chatter of loved ones, I felt a sense of peace wash over me. Home, truly, was where the heart was, and in that moment, surrounded by the ones I loved, I couldn't have been happier.

Back home, Diwali buzzed with laughter, sweets, and family gatherings. As the fireworks lit up the night sky, I couldn't contain my excitement as I unwrapped the gift from my father—a sleek Samsung phone.

"Wow, Papa! This is amazing!" I exclaimed, holding the device in awe.

"I knew you'd like it, *beta*. You've been working so hard," my father replied with a smile, his eyes reflecting pride.

Amidst the Diwali celebrations, my relatives gathered around, showering me with congratulations and titles like "Engineer Saheb."

"Congratulations, Engineer Saheb! You'll go far," one uncle exclaimed, patting me on the back. "Thank you, uncle," I replied, feeling a mix of pride and unease at the unfamiliar title.

Later, as we sat down for dinner, the conversation took an unexpected turn when one of my relatives broached the topic of marriage. Relatives, especially the older ones like Phupha Ji and Mausa Ji, in UP, are often fixated on one thing: marriage. According to them, once a boy enrols in an Engineering College, he becomes the most eligible bachelor. They believe that all the money spent on his education should now be a burden for the girl's family, eventually making it their moral responsibility to find a suitable match. The prevailing idea is that if they can secure a good match for the boy, they'll earn the family's gratitude and respect forever.

Let me clarify what they mean by a "suitable match". It usually refers to a girl whose parents are willing to pay a handsome dowry. The more extravagant the wedding, the greater the expectations placed on these relatives. They seem to think that the flashier the event, the more obligations they've earned. It's a tangled web of tradition and expectation, where love and compatibility take a backseat to status and wealth.

"Have you thought about your future, *beta*? You're an engineer now, it's time to start thinking about settling down," my aunt remarked, her words tinged with expectation.

I shifted uncomfortably in my seat, unsure of how to respond to such a weighty question. The expectations placed on me felt suffocating, leaving me grappling with conflicting emotions amidst the festive cheer. I soon started regretting my decision to spend these crucial seven days back home. Even though I knew my exams were approaching just a month away, the thought of reuniting with my parents had drawn me back. Little did I expect to be greeted with the saccharine yet suffocating words of relatives who had bestowed upon me the title of "Engineer Saheb"—without me even holding a degree. As if that wasn't enough, some of them had the cheek to propose potential brides for me! The whole experience was both disgusting and alarming. It was overwhelming to face such expectations when all I wanted was a peaceful break, not to be thrust into the whirlwind of marriage talks and societal pressure.

As the night wore on, I found myself caught between the warmth of family love and the pressure of societal norms, longing for a sense of belonging in a world that seemed to be moving too fast

******

6. Cheers to Chaos: Navigating Exam Season

The campus was buzzing as students trickled back after the short vacation. Some looked refreshed, while others—like me, Raj, and Rahul—carried the burden of the looming exams on our shoulders. The break was supposed to help, but now it felt like it had just delayed the inevitable.

"I thought the break would calm me down, but it feels like I've forgotten everything," Rahul groaned as we walked to the dorm.

Raj smirked. "I went through my notes last night, and I swear half of them looked like ancient hieroglyphs."

I kept quiet, but the same anxiety gnawed at me. Despite spending hours preparing, the pile of study material seemed insurmountable. The exams were just a few days away, and my brain felt like it was about to explode.

Just as we stepped into the dorm, a loud burst of laughter echoed from the common room. And there he was—Krishav, back on campus, swaggering like he had all the time in the world. He'd returned 10 days after the break was over, with only a handful of days left until the exams. Of course, he looked unfazed. His flashy jacket, expensive watch, and relaxed grin screamed, "No worries."

Raj muttered, "Look who's finally graced us with his presence."

Krishav dumped his bags on the couch with a dramatic sigh. "Boys! Miss me? Manali was a blast. You should've seen the slopes! And the parties? Legendary. Studying? That can wait."

I couldn't stay quiet anymore. "Krishav, the exams are in a few days. Don't you think you should at least pretend to care?"

Krishav shrugged, completely nonchalant. "Dude, these exams are a formality. I'll figure it out like always. Why stress?"

We exchanged glances, unable to comprehend how someone could be so carefree. For us, these exams were everything—our futures, our families, and the fear of failure. For Krishav? It was just another bump in his effortlessly smooth road.

"Speaking of not stressing," Krishav said, reaching into his bag, "I've got something to help you guys relax." He pulled out a six-pack of beer. "Behold—the magic potion that'll boost your exam performance!"

Rahul was the first to grab a bottle, downing it in record time. "Ah, liquid courage," he said, wiping his mouth. "That's better."

And then his phone rang. He groaned, checking the screen. "It's my mom, probably asking if I've packed to head home after I fail."

I laughed. "Tell her to save me a seat on that train."

He silenced his phone, and the beer bottle made its way to Raj, who waved it off. "No thanks, I'd rather be hungover after I fail, not before."

Mohit, sitting quietly on the couch, hesitated for a moment before grabbing the bottle with a grin. "Well, if we're going down, might as well do it with style."

Krishav handed a bottle to me. I hesitated but took a sip. Why not? It's not like panicking was going to help.

As we relaxed, Krishav leaned in with a mischievous look. "Okay, time for a joke. But fair warning, it's a little... spicy."

We all leaned in, knowing Krishav's jokes were always ridiculous but somehow exactly what we needed.

"Alright," he began, "So, a student walks into an exam hall late, sits down next to his friend and whispers, 'I'm totally screwed, man. I forgot to study.' His friend, looking completely calm, says, 'Don't worry, neither did I.' The first guy, panicking, asks, 'Then how are you so relaxed?' His friend shrugs and says, 'Well, I figure if I fail, I'll just marry someone rich. That's Plan B.'"

He paused dramatically, grinning. "And the first guy goes, 'What's Plan A?' And his friend says, 'I'm still working on that. But Plan B's pretty solid, don't you think?'"

The room exploded with laughter. Mohit snorted beer out of his nose, while Raj nearly choked.

Rahul wiped his eyes, gasping for air. "I swear, only you, Krishav. Only you."

Once we calmed down, Krishav decided to kick things up a notch. "Let's play a game—'Exam Jeopardy.' Every wrong answer means you take a chug. I'll quiz you."

Raj groaned. "This is going to end terribly."

Krishav grinned. "Exactly. First question: What's Newton's third law?"

Mohit squirmed, clearly blanking out. "Uh... something about motion?"

"Wrong!" Krishav shouted, laughing as he handed Mohit the bottle. "Chug!"

It didn't take long for the game to spiral out of control. Every wrong answer led to more drinks, more laughter, and less studying. Before long, Rahul was slumped on the couch, his face turning an interesting shade of green. "Guys," he said weakly, "I think I went too hard on the 'magic potion.'"

And then, just like that, he bolted out of the room. The door slammed shut behind him, leaving us in stunned silence for a beat—before we all burst into hysterical laughter.

"Did Rahul just run off to puke mid-sentence?" I gasped, clutching my sides.

Krishav, barely containing himself, nodded. "Guess the 'potion' wasn't so magical after all."

Rahul stumbled back into the room a few minutes later, looking worse for wear but managing a sheepish grin. "Never again," he muttered, collapsing onto the couch.

Krishav, still grinning, raised his empty bottle in a mock toast. "To Rahul—may you never challenge the 'magic potion' again!"

The mood lightened after that. Even though we hadn't touched our books, the tension that had been suffocating us for weeks felt a little less overwhelming. Krishav might've been a carefree goof, but for a moment, I couldn't help but agree with him—sometimes you just had to laugh your way through the stress.

As the night wore on, we finally cracked open our notes, though the seriousness of the exams still lingered in the background. Krishav, of course, didn't even glance at a book, but somehow, it didn't seem to matter. The storm of exams was coming, and we all knew it. But now, thanks to Krishav's ridiculous jokes, the beers, and the chaos that unfolded, it felt a little less terrifying.

******

6. From Books to Banquets: Celebrating Krishav's Success

Finally, the examination was over, the air was thick with anticipation as we all anxiously awaited our exam results. It was time for fun and frolics. The tension was palpable, and even the usually boisterous chatter in the dorms was subdued. To our collective astonishment, even Krishav managed to pass. This was the guy who spent more time perfecting his cricket swing than cracking open a textbook. We half-expected the professors to hold a press conference to verify his results. But miracles do happen, and Krishav's success was the proof. His dad caught up in the rare glow of paternal pride, decided to treat us all to a fancy meal at Sayaji Continental, a swanky five-star hotel that was a world away from our usual haunt, the campus canteen.

The evening of the dinner at Sayaji Continental felt like stepping into a scene from a glamorous movie, except I was the clumsy extra trying not to trip over my own feet. As we walked into the grand lobby, adorned with sparkling chandeliers and the fragrance of exotic flowers, I couldn't shake off the feeling of being a fish out of water. The sheer opulence of the place was both awe-inspiring and intimidating, making me question whether my usual go-to meal of instant noodles would be deemed appropriate etiquette for such a lavish setting.

Amidst the overwhelming ambience, my excitement was eclipsed by a hefty dose of nervousness. Thoughts raced through my mind like a hyperactive squirrel on caffeine: What if I used the wrong fork? What if I pronounced the dish names incorrectly? I couldn't help but chuckle at the absurdity of it all. Here we were, a ragtag group of students who had once celebrated passing exams with instant noodles, suddenly thrust into the lap of luxury. I stole a glance at Krishav, who was striding confidently forward as if he had been born to dine in such extravagant surroundings. "Who knew passing exams could be this rewarding?" I whispered to my friend next to me, barely able to suppress a laugh.

The whole experience felt like a delightful mix of the unfamiliar and the absurd, and as the night progressed, we found ourselves gradually relaxing and relishing this unexpected taste of the high life.

At the start of the second semester, the subjects loomed over me like Mount Everest, and I felt like a climber without ropes. Thermodynamics and Engineering Drawing were the toughest peaks. Freehand drawing, Rankine Cycle, Carnot Cycle, pumps, pistons, condensers, engines—you name it, I struggled with it. The technical jargon sounded like a foreign language, and my notes resembled hieroglyphics.

Just when I was convinced that I was doomed to become a permanent resident of the campus library, Dev entered the picture. Dev was a wizard with Engineering Drawing, turning complex schematics into works of art with ease. He offered to help me out, and for a while, it seemed like there was a glimmer of hope. But fate had other plans. Despite our combined efforts and countless late-night study sessions fuelled by caffeine and desperation, I couldn't crack two subjects this semester.

Even Rahul, my rock and the one person who always seemed to have it together, couldn't make it through. When he decided to throw in the towel and head home, it felt like the ground beneath me crumbled. Rahul's departure hit me hard, like losing my compass in a storm. Without his steady presence, my frustration grew. I began to resent engineering with a passion. The irony of it all struck me—here I was, trying to engineer my future, but it felt like my future was engineering my downfall. Yet, fear held me back from making a change. What if I wasn't cut out for anything else? The thought of switching majors or dropping out entirely filled me with dread. So, I continued to wrestle with my textbooks and lecture notes, hoping against hope that I would somehow find my footing before it was too late.

"Bound by Dreams, Fuelled by Pressure"

In the dawn of dreams, I stood with pride,
Engineering, my passion, my guide.
Yet Thermodynamics' complex sway,
Turned my fervour to dismay.

Engineering Drawing's subtle lines,
Entangled hopes in intricate designs.
Rahul's departure, a bitter blow,
Left my spirit lost, sinking low.

To quit now, seemed tempting,
But society's whispers I couldn't ignore.
"Kya kahenge log?" echoed within,
Binding me tight, though I yearned to begin.

I could clearly see my father's gift,
the expensive Samsung phone,
Words of relatives, all the respect that I had known.
It was all because of this engineering path,
How could I even think of facing their wrath?

So, I wrestle with pages, notes in hand,
Hoping one day I'll understand.
Against the tide, I fight and strive,
Seeking my footing, to keep dreams alive.

******

7. Cracking the Code: The Mystery of Krishav's Success

To everyone's shock, Krishav effortlessly sailed through his exams yet again this semester, leaving us in a state of awe mingled with a tinge of envy. His consistent success sparked a mixture of admiration and curiosity in our hearts, prompting me to become more determined than ever to uncover his secret to academic prowess.

With Rahul's absence leaving a void in our study group, I found myself gravitating towards Krishav more often, eager to unravel the mystery behind his achievements. His cool and carefree demeanour only added to the intrigue. How could someone who seemed to spend more time on the cricket field and at late-night hangouts than in the library consistently excel in academics?

Highs Lows

As I observed Krishav's relaxed approach to life juxtaposed with his academic achievements, I couldn't help but feel baffled yet charmed. While the rest of us would spend hours buried in our books, grappling with complex formulas and diagrams, Krishav seemed to effortlessly clear his papers with minimal effort. It was as if he possessed some elusive secret recipe for success, a hidden formula or magic trick that gave him an edge in the academic arena. And so, fuelled by determination and curiosity, I embarked on a mission to uncover the truth behind Krishav's effortless triumphs.

Spending time with Krishav was like a rollercoaster ride of emotions, swinging between sheer amusement and mild frustration. His nonchalant attitude towards challenging subjects never failed to elicit laughter from me. "Thermodynamics? Just think of it as a hot cup of chai cooling down," he would quip, accompanied by a playful wink. His ability to distil complex concepts into simple, relatable analogies was both baffling and intriguing. Behind the humour, however, lay a burning desire to unravel his method. Perhaps it was his innate talent for making everything appear simpler than it truly was. Or maybe his secret lay in his unwavering calmness under pressure—a skill that seemed to elude me entirely.

Despite Krishav's continued success, there was a noticeable shift in his demeanour this time around. Gone was the jubilant celebration that usually accompanied his triumphs. Instead, his victory was marked by a quiet humility, almost as if he had learned a lesson in humility from the universe or sensed the growing frustration among his friends. As I observed him from afar, I couldn't help but feel an even deeper sense of curiosity about the enigmatic approach that kept him consistently ahead of the curve. As I struggled with my own studies, I found myself yearning for a fraction of Krishav's carefree confidence, hoping that some of it would eventually rub off on me.

Me: "Hey Krishav, how do you manage to stay so calm during exams? I feel like I'm always on the verge of a nervous breakdown."

Krishav, flashing a grin: "Oh, exams are like cricket matches, mate. You just gotta keep your cool, focus on the game plan, and trust in your abilities. And hey, if all else fails, there's always chai to soothe the nerves!"

Dev, who was observing me getting close to Krishav, did not like this idea. He warned me to keep away from him, sensing the potential dangers ahead. His words echoed in the back of my mind like a persistent alarm clock, but I was too enamoured with Krishav's laid-back charm to pay them much heed. Perhaps Dev sensed my growing infatuation with Krishav and the potential threats it posed. He tried to steer me back onto the path of righteousness, offering words of encouragement and urging me to believe in myself. Yet, like a stubborn bull with blinders on, I brushed off his concerns, too entranced by Krishav's magnetic pull.

Looking back, maybe that's why Dev acted the way he did at his birthday party when you introduced me to him, Richa. His eyes held a mixture of disappointment and concern as he watched me laugh and joke with Krishav, oblivious to the warnings he had tried so hard to convey. Despite his efforts to protect me from veering off course, I was too blinded by the allure of Krishav's carefree attitude. I wish I could then see the storm that was brewing beneath the surface, waiting to shake the foundations of our friendship and teach me a lesson in trust and loyalty."

******

8. Dorm Drift: Friendship Fluctuations

In the bustling world of college life, my room was a hub of activity, where friends from different backgrounds and interests converged. While Vengadesh and Avaneesh preferred the serene confines of Aryabhatta hostel for their study sessions, Rahul and Raj, fellow Mechanical enthusiasts, found it more homelike in the familiar surroundings of my room. Together, we formed an eclectic group, united by our shared passion for learning and camaraderie. Our study sessions were more than just academic pursuits; they were vibrant exchanges of ideas and debates that fuelled our intellectual curiosity.

Rahul, with his fervent admiration for Mr Modi and his keen interest in politics, was like a live wire, constantly sparking lively discussions that could rival any parliamentary debate. His enthusiasm was infectious, drawing us all into the realm of political discourse, whether we liked it or not. With a mischievous glint in his eye, he would launch into passionate monologues extolling the virtues of his political idol, leaving no stone unturned in his efforts to convert us to his cause. But for every point Rahul made, there was Raj, the resident sceptic, ready to pounce with his own brand of wit and sarcasm. Their debates were legendary, a clash of ideologies that turned our study sessions into veritable battlegrounds of intellect and humour.

Amidst the chaos of debates and discussions, Dev's presence served as a comforting anchor in our group. His easy-going nature and genuine interest in our academic pursuits brought a sense of warmth to and trust in our interactions. With each shared moment, Dev became a cherished companion, someone whose company we all valued deeply. However, with Rahul's departure, the vibrant dynamic of our group underwent a noticeable shift. The once bustling atmosphere of my room grew quiet, the absence of our spirited debates leaving a palpable void in the air. Even Dev, usually so affable and engaged, seemed lost in his own thoughts, his presence tinged with a hint of melancholy.

Feeling the weight of Rahul's absence keenly, I made the bold decision to seek companionship elsewhere, convincing Krishav to share his room with me. It was a leap into the unknown, a decision driven by a sense of longing for the fellowship and lively banter that had once filled our room. Who knew that this simple choice would mark the beginning of a new chapter in my college journey, one filled with unexpected twists and turns? As I embarked on this new adventure, I couldn't help but feel a mix of apprehension and excitement, wondering what the future held in store for me and my newfound roommate.

******

9. Glamour and Envy: Krishav's Birthday Bash

On the 23rd of April, Krishav's birthday bash became the hottest topic on our college campus, sparking gossip and excitement among students. Held at a nearby restaurant, the event was nothing short of a spectacle, with Krishav's charismatic personality and affluent status ensuring a grand affair. As we entered the venue, it felt like stepping into a different world altogether, one where lavish decorations and pulsating music set the stage for an unforgettable night. Amidst the glitz and glamour, Krishav seemed to glide through the crowd with the grace of a seasoned performer, effortlessly charming everyone in his path.

HIGHS LOWS

Yet amidst the festivities, a twinge of jealousy couldn't help but creep into our hearts as we watched Krishav bask in the spotlight. His effortless charm seemed to attract not only attention but also admiration, particularly from the fairer sex. As we observed him effortlessly navigate through the crowd, surrounded by a bevy of admirers, we couldn't help but feel a pang of envy. After all, while Krishav may have been living in his own realm of luxury and privilege, the rest of us couldn't help but feel like mere spectators in comparison.

Amidst the lively celebration, Krishav decided to play matchmaker and introduced me to Pari, one of the topper students in our batch. Her name wasn't just a coincidence; she truly embodied the ethereal beauty of a fairy. With a smile that could brighten the gloomiest of days and eyes that shimmered with intelligence, she captivated everyone in her presence. Meeting her felt like stumbling upon a rare gem in a sea of ordinary stones, and I found myself instantly drawn to her magnetic charm.

As I stood next to Krishav, basking in Pari's radiant aura, I couldn't help but marvel at his endless luck. Here was a man who had managed to win over not just one, but two of the most coveted prizes in our college: academic excellence and the heart of a beautiful girl. It was as if luck and charm were woven into his very being, effortlessly guiding him through life's twists and turns. And yet, amidst my admiration for Krishav's good fortune, I couldn't shake off the faint whisper of envy that lingered in the depths of my heart.

As the night progressed, I found myself entangled in a web of conflicting emotions, oscillating between admiration for Krishav's apparently enchanted existence and a subtle tinge of envy for all that he effortlessly possessed. It was a surreal experience, being in the presence of someone who appeared to have life's puzzle pieces effortlessly fall into place. However, amidst the glitz and glamour of Krishav's birthday bash, I couldn't shake the nagging feeling that perhaps there was more to life than just material wealth and superficial charm.

As I observed Krishav and Pari dance gracefully amidst the swirling lights and pulsating music, I couldn't help but wonder if their seemingly perfect facade concealed deeper complexities and struggles. Behind their smiles and flawless exteriors, I questioned whether they too grappled with doubts and insecurities. Was true happiness merely a mirage in the midst of such superficiality? The night's festivities seemed to blur the lines between reality and illusion, leaving me pondering the elusive nature of fulfilment and the quest for authenticity in a world enamoured by appearances.

****

10. Golden Bonds: Friendship and Ambition

Pari's friendship was indeed the unexpected treasure from Krishav's birthday festivities. She possessed a heart of pure gold, radiating warmth and kindness in every interaction. Her genuine concern for Krishav's well-being often led to our frequent conversations, bridging the gap between acquaintances and transforming us into confidants. It was almost comical how I became the unofficial Krishav tracker, receiving calls from Pari whenever Krishav went off the radar, which, let's be honest, was quite often. I hardly knew that these trivial calls would blossom into a friendship that would change the course of my college life.

Highs Lows

As our conversations became more frequent and meaningful, Pari's presence became a constant source of comfort and support. Despite being the topper of our section, she never hesitated to lend a helping hand whenever I stumbled over academic hurdles. Our encounters in the canteen and library became cherished moments of amity and shared laughter, where she effortlessly balanced her academic prowess with her innate kindness. It was almost as if she had a magical ability to simplify even the most daunting of subjects, making the third semester feel like a gentle breeze rather than a raging storm.

Through our growing friendship, I learned that Pari hailed from Kanpur, a detail that seemed insignificant at first but soon became a thread that connected our pasts. It was a delightful revelation to discover that we had shared a bus ride back home after our first semester examinations. In Pari, I found not just a friend, but a kindred spirit whose presence illuminated even the darkest corners of my college experience. With her by my side, the challenges of academia seemed less daunting, and the journey through the maze of textbooks and lectures became an adventure rather than a chore.

As we shared more about our family backgrounds, Pari confided in me about her humble origins, belonging to a family of farmers. Her ambitions shone brightly in her eyes as she spoke of her desire to make her father proud, a man who had sacrificed so much for her education.

Through her words, I glimpsed the depth of her determination and the unwavering love she held for her family, inspiring me to strive for excellence in my own pursuits. The bond we shared went beyond mere friendship; it was a connection forged in mutual respect, understanding, and a shared commitment to achieving our dreams.

Our connection ran deeper than mere study sessions; it was a bond forged in the fires of shared dreams, fears, and aspirations. Pari was not just a study buddy; she was a confidante, a beacon of light in the darkness of college life. In moments of vulnerability, I found myself yearning for someone like her—a constant source of support and positivity. With her trademark smile, she would gently steer me back on track, reminding me to focus on the present and trust that the future would unfold as it should. Her words were like a soothing balm to my frazzled nerves, calming the storm raging within.

Pari's laughter was infectious, filling even the most mundane moments with joy and laughter. The sound of her laughter echoed through the corridors of our friendship, bringing warmth and light to even the darkest of days. In those shared laughs, I found comfort, a reminder that amidst the chaos of deadlines and exams, there was always room for laughter and lightness. Her presence filled the gaps left by the absence of Rahul and Raj, bringing a sense of wholeness to our shared experiences.

HIGHS LOWS

As our friendship blossomed, I couldn't shake off the nagging feeling that something had shifted between Pari and Krishav. Their once lively connection seemed to dim, replaced by an unsettling silence that hung heavily in the air whenever they were together. Even my interactions with Krishav took on a strained quality, his usual warmth replaced by a distant demeanour. It was like tiptoeing through a minefield of unspoken tension, each step fraught with the fear of igniting a dormant spark of conflict. Despite our efforts to maintain a facade of normalcy, the palpable awkwardness lingered like a heavy cloud, casting a shadow over our once-carefree interactions.

Yet, amidst the discomfort and uncertainty, I found uncanny relief in the presence of Pari by my side. Her steadfast support and genuine concern served as a beacon of light in the midst of the storm, guiding me through the murky waters of our strained friendships. As our bond deepened, I came to realise that true friendship transcends the boundaries of time and space, anchoring us in a sea of uncertainty with the unwavering promise of companionship and understanding. In Pari's unwavering loyalty, I found the strength to navigate the turbulent currents of our shifting dynamics, grateful for the steady anchor she provided in the tumultuous sea of our college years.

******

11. Dorm Drama: Betrayal and Blowback

One fateful night, as the moon cast its ethereal glow upon our dormitory, I found myself unwittingly thrust into a storm of betrayal and misunderstanding. The air was heavy with the scent of alcohol, a bitter reminder of the intoxicating haze that clouded Krishav's judgement as he unleashed a torrent of accusations against Pari. His drunken ramblings painted a grim picture of betrayal and deceit, insinuating an illicit affair between Pari and myself. Though his words were slurred and his mind clouded by inebriation, each accusation struck me like a dagger to the heart, leaving me reeling in disbelief and confusion. In that moment, the weight of Krishav's accusations threatened to suffocate me, as I struggled to make sense of the chaos unfolding around us.

As the accusations hung in the air like a dark cloud, I realised the gravity of the situation: Krishav's trust in our friendship had been shattered, and I was left grappling with the devastating aftermath of his unfounded suspicions. The bond that once held us together now lay fractured, the foundation of our friendship crumbling beneath the weight of betrayal and misunderstanding. With each passing moment, the rift between us widened, threatening to swallow us whole in a vortex of mistrust and resentment. In the face of such turmoil, I was left with no choice but to confront the harsh reality of our shattered friendship, and the daunting task of rebuilding what had been lost amidst the wreckage of Krishav's accusations.

As I tried to reason with Krishav, my words fell upon deaf ears, drowned out by his drunken tirade against Pari. Yet, amidst his accusations and unfounded suspicions, a glimmer of truth emerged: our friendship was not born out of romantic entanglement, but rather out of a shared sense of insecurity and longing for connection. Krishav's neglect of Pari had fuelled her insecurity, driving her to seek refuge in our friendship. It was a delicate balance, fraught with unspoken tensions and unfulfilled desires, yet it bound us together in a bond forged by mutual understanding and support.

Krishav's behaviour was undeniably flawed; his failure to consider Pari's feelings and his flirtatious bearing with other girls only amplified her insecurities. However, it was his cruel words that cut deep. As he hurled insults at her family and hometown, tarnishing her character and upbringing with baseless accusations, a surge of indignation rose within me. How dare he belittle her and sully her reputation with such venomous vitriol?

In a moment of righteous fury, I could no longer contain my anger. With a swift blow to his mouth, I silenced his hurtful words, the resounding smack echoing through the room like a thunderclap. It was a visceral response, driven by a primal instinct to defend Pari's honour and protect her from further harm. Yet, as the weight of my actions settled upon me, I realised that violence was not the answer. Despite my righteous intentions, I had succumbed to the same destructive impulses that had fuelled Krishav's outburst, and in doing so, I had only added fuel to the fire of our escalating conflict.

In the aftermath of our confrontation, as the echoes of our argument faded into the night, I found myself engulfed in a sea of emotions. Anger, frustration, and regret churned within me, their tempestuous currents threatening to overwhelm my senses. Yet, amidst the chaos of my inner turmoil, a glimmer of hope persisted— a beacon of light in the darkness of our strained relationship.

Beneath the layers of hurt and resentment lay a flicker of optimism, fuelled by the belief that through open communication and genuine understanding, we could navigate the rocky terrain of our fractured friendship and emerge stronger than before. Despite the wounds inflicted by our heated exchange, I clung to the notion that honesty and empathy could serve as the catalysts for healing, forging a path towards reconciliation and mutual forgiveness. It was a daunting journey fraught with uncertainty, but as I faced the challenges that lay ahead, I resolved to confront them with courage and resilience, guided by the unwavering belief that even the deepest rifts could be bridged with patience and goodwill.

******

12. Paths to Reconciliation

The morning after the stormy confrontation, a sense of urgency gripped me as I realised the gravity of the situation. The events of the previous night had set in motion a chain of consequences that could irreparably damage the delicate fabric of our friendship. With a heavy heart and a determination to set things right, I made my way to Krishav's bed, steeling myself for the conversation that lay ahead. As I stood before him, I felt a knot of apprehension tighten in my stomach. Would he react with anger and hostility, or would he, like me, recognize the need for reconciliation and understanding? With a deep breath, I folded my hands and offered a sincere apology for my actions, hoping against hope that Krishav would meet my gesture of contrition with forgiveness and understanding.

To my immense relief, Krishav's response was not one of anger or resentment, but rather of surprising maturity and understanding. His willingness to let bygones be bygones and move forward filled me with a sense of gratitude and admiration. In that moment, I realised the true depth of our friendship, forged in the crucible of shared experiences and mutual respect.

With a tight hug and a few reassuring words, I conveyed my earnest plea for Krishav to mend the rift between him and Pari. It was a plea born out of genuine concern for both of them, a desire to see them reunited and happy once more. And to my immense relief, Krishav consented, his willingness to make amends a testament to the strength of our bond and the power of forgiveness.

As I left Krishav's side, a sense of peace washed over me, replacing the earlier turmoil with a renewed sense of hope and optimism. In that moment of reconciliation, I thanked whatever higher power had intervened to guide us through the darkness and into the light. As I watched Krishav and Pari embark on a journey of healing and forgiveness, I knew that no matter what challenges lay ahead, we would face them together, united in friendship and bound by the ties that bind us.

That very evening, as I glanced across the café and saw Pari and Krishav engrossed in conversation, a wave of relief washed over me. The sight of them laughing and chatting together filled me with a sense of satisfaction, knowing that my efforts to reconcile them had borne fruit. It was a moment of quiet triumph, a reminder that even amidst the chaos of misunderstandings and miscommunications, harmony could be restored.

Yet, as I watched them from afar, a pang of apprehension gnawed at my heart. The memory of the previous night's turmoil lingered, a stark reminder of the fragility of relationships and the importance of maintaining boundaries. Determined to prevent any recurrence of misunderstanding, I resolved to keep a respectful distance from Pari, allowing her and Krishav the space they needed to rebuild their bond.

With a heavy heart, I concocted a plan to distance myself from the situation, convincing Krishav that my studies required me to seek assistance from Raj in the Aryabhatta hostel. It was a white lie born out of necessity, a means to safeguard the fragile peace that had been restored. Despite Raj's initial reluctance, I implored him to lend me his company for studies, knowing that his support would be invaluable in the upcoming examinations. In the end, he relented, agreeing to assist me in my academic endeavours, albeit begrudgingly.

In the days following the upheaval in my life, I grappled with some uncontrolled emotions, struggling to come to terms with the sudden change that had turned my world upside down. It wasn't easy to accept the new reality thrust upon me, but with each passing day, I found myself slowly adapting to my altered circumstances. The weight of impending examinations loomed over me like a dark cloud, but with the unwavering support of Raj and Dev by my side, I found the strength to soldier on.

Despite my best efforts to move forward, occasional calls from Krishav and Pari served as painful reminders of the tumultuous events that had transpired. Each ring of the phone dredged up memories of the past, threatening to unravel the fragile peace I had worked so hard to restore. Yet, in those moments of vulnerability, I drew strength from the knowledge that I was not alone. Pari's unwavering support and understanding served as a beacon of hope, a reminder that I was not defined by the suspicions of others.

With each passing day, I grew stronger, fortified by the bonds of friendship and the resilience of the human spirit. I had confided in Pari about the events of that fateful night, and her willingness to stand by me in the face of adversity only strengthened our connection. Together, we navigated the choppy waters of uncertainty, determined to emerge unscathed on the other side. And though the road ahead was fraught with challenges, I knew that as long as I had the support of my friends and the courage to face whatever came my way, I would emerge victorious in the end.

******

13. Love: Life-time Pain

The morning began like any other until an unexpected call from Krishav disrupted the tranquillity of my day. His inquiry about my exam preparations caught me off guard, as it was unusual for him to reach out so early in the morning with such a mundane question. Despite my initial surprise, I assured him that my studies were progressing satisfactorily, albeit with a few hurdles in Advanced Mathematics and Workshop Technology. Only if I knew that this innocuous conversation would set in motion a chain of events that would alter the course of my life.

As the day wore on, Raj's stern warning echoed in my mind, urging me to heed his advice and steer clear of Krishav's invitation. Yet, a stubborn resolve gnawed at my conscience, tempting me to defy Raj's cautionary words and meet Krishav as planned. Ignoring the voice of reason, I brushed aside Raj's concerns and made my way to the restaurant where Krishav had celebrated his birthday, unaware of the dangers that lay ahead.

In hindsight, my decision to disregard Raj's warning proved to be a grave mistake, one that would have far-reaching consequences. I wish I knew that this seemingly innocent rendezvous would plunge me into the depth of deception and betrayal, shattering the fragile peace I had worked so hard to maintain. As I reflect on that fateful evening, I can't help but rue the choices that led me down this treacherous path, longing for the chance to turn back the hands of time and undo the mistakes that cost me dearly.

As I stepped into the familiar confines of the café, my heart clenched at the sight of Pari, her usual effervescent spirit dimmed by an unmistakable veil of distress. Concern etched deep into my features, I approached her cautiously, the weight of worry heavy on my shoulders.

"Hey, Pari... Are you okay?" I murmured softly; my voice tinged with apprehension.

Attempting to mask her turmoil behind a facade of false cheer, Pari offered me a strained smile. "What a coincidence! You... here!" she replied, her words falling flat against the backdrop of her unshed tears. Sensing her discomfort, I tried to ease the tension, affirming my presence with a simple "Yes," hoping to provide some semblance of comfort in her time of need.

As we exchanged pleasantries, I couldn't shake the feeling that something was amiss. Pari's attempts to deflect my concern only served to heighten my unease, prompting me to inquire about Krishav's whereabouts. At that moment, the floodgates of emotion burst open, and Pari's fragile facade crumbled before my eyes. Tears streamed down her cheeks as she confessed, "I-I haven't seen

Krishav for a week or so... He won't even talk to me anymore..." Her voice quivered with raw emotion, a haunting echo of the pain she bore deep within her soul.

My heart clenched at the raw vulnerability in her words, her pain echoing in every tear that streamed down her cheeks. It was heart-wrenching to see her in such a fragile state, her usual effervescent charm dimmed by the weight of her turmoil. As I watched Pari's tears fall, a wave of empathy washed over me, and I couldn't help but speak to myself, albeit softly, almost as if whispering a warning to my own heart. "If this is the result of loving someone so desperately," I mused, my words tinged with a hint of resignation, "I had better never gotten caught into the trap called love."

I reached out, offering whatever comfort I could muster as I struggled to find the right words. "I'm here for you, Pari," I murmured softly, wrapping an arm around her trembling shoulders. "You're not alone in this. We'll get through it together."

But deep down, I knew that this entangled relationship was taking its toll on her in more ways than one. The thought of how it might impact her academic performance gnawed at me, filling me with a sense of urgency to help her find a resolution.

Despite the unease gnawing at my insides, I resolved to stay by her side, offering my support as we awaited Krishav's arrival, clinging to the hope that perhaps, together, we could untangle the knots of misunderstanding and find a glimmer of peace amidst the chaos.

******

14. Broken Trust: The Cost of Ignoring Warning Signs

As I waited anxiously for Krishav's arrival, each passing minute felt like an eternity, my nerves fraying with every unanswered call. Frustration mingled with apprehension as I contemplated the unsettling silence on the other end of the line. Just as I was on the verge of abandoning hope, a stranger approached, bearing a mysterious blue polybag purportedly from Krishav. With trembling hands, I tore open the bag, only to be met with a chilling sight—a stack of Advanced Mathematics exam papers and a wad of cash. Confusion and dread gripped my heart as I struggled to comprehend the implications of this ominous delivery.

Panic surged through me like a tidal wave as the gravity of the situation sank in. With trembling hands and racing thoughts, we made the decision to alert the proctor immediately, desperate to unravel the mystery surrounding Krishav's inexplicable disappearance. As we hurriedly made our way to the authorities, several emotions churned within me—fear, uncertainty, and a gnawing sense of betrayal. This unsettling turn of events was just the beginning of a tormenting journey full of danger and deceit.

Pari's composure shattered at the breach of trust, her anguish evident in uncontrollable wails as she grappled with the impending disaster. Despite my attempts at pacification, her distress only deepened, each sob a testament to the betrayal weighing heavily upon her. Her tears mirrored the shattered expectations and shattered dreams, echoing the profound sense of helplessness that enveloped us both. In the midst of this turmoil, I pledged unwavering support, determined to stand by her side as we navigated the storm of betrayal together, emerging stronger in the face of adversity. Pari's distress spurred us into action, and with a shared sense of urgency, we swiftly made our way to the proctor's office, determined to uncover the truth behind Krishav's disappearance and the ominous package he had left behind.

As we approached the college gate, a knot of apprehension tightened in my stomach, the weight of uncertainty bearing down upon us like a leaden cloak. The atmosphere crackled with tension, anticipation mingling with dread as we braced ourselves for the inevitable confrontation that lay ahead. With each passing moment, the air grew thicker, suffused with a palpable sense of foreboding that seemed to cling to us like a shroud.

The sight of the hostel warden and chief proctor standing before us sent a chill down my spine, their stern expressions offering no reassurance in the face of impending judgment. My heart raced as I struggled to find the right words, my mind racing with thoughts of the repercussions that awaited us. It was as if time stood still, frozen in a moment of suspended animation, as we stood before the authorities, our fate hanging in the balance.

Before I could even utter a single word, the proctor's swift action seized the damning evidence from my trembling hand, his accusatory gaze stripping away any semblance of innocence. At that moment, I felt a wave of despair wash over me, the weight of guilt and betrayal threatening to crush me beneath its relentless tide. Yet amidst the chaos of emotions, a glimmer of determination flickered to life within me, a resolve to confront the consequences of our actions head-on, no matter the cost.

"What is the meaning of this?" he demanded; his voice sharp with contempt. "Explain yourselves!"

I tried to speak, to plead our innocence, but my words were drowned out by the proctor's tirade. Pari's tears flowed freely, her cries echoing in the cold, unforgiving air. My heart ached at the sight of her pain, the weight of injustice bearing down upon us like a crushing weight.

"P-Please, sir, you must listen," Pari implored, her voice quivering with emotion as she stepped forward, her eyes pleading for understanding. "We are not guilty of any wrongdoing." But her heartfelt plea seemed to fall on deaf ears as the proctor's relentless assault continued unabated.

"So, this is how you managed to top the college, Ms. Topper!" the proctor sneered, his tone laced with disdain as he levelled accusations against us. "I always knew these dogs of small cities; they cannot excel without resorting to unfair means." His harsh words cut through the air like a knife, leaving wounds that seemed impossible to heal.

Amidst the chaos and turmoil, my gaze fell upon Krishav, his smug demeanour serving as a painful reminder of the trap he had laid for us. Anger surged within me, mingling with a deep sense of betrayal at his betrayal. How could he have orchestrated such a cruel scheme, sacrificing our reputations for his own gain? The realisation struck me like a physical blow, fuelling a burning resolve to seek justice and expose his treachery for all to see.

"It was him," I whispered to Pari, my voice barely audible, above the din. "Krishav set us up."

The realisation hit me like a blow to the chest, filling me with a mix of rage and despair. I felt the weight of injustice pressing down upon us, threatening to crush us beneath its unforgiving grip. And yet, amidst the darkness, a glimmer of hope flickered—a determination to fight against the cruelty and injustice that threatened to consume us.

Meanwhile, the proctor asked us to submit our explanation within a week and to meet him in his office with our parents. As the weight of the proctor's ultimatum settled upon us like a heavy burden, the prospect of facing our parents loomed before us like an insurmountable obstacle. The thought of confessing our predicament to them filled me with dread, knowing the disappointment and worry it would surely elicit. Yet, amidst the turmoil, my primary concern lay with Pari, whose devastation threatened to engulf her completely. With each passing moment, I felt the weight of her anguish pressing down upon me, a constant reminder of the fragile state of her mental and emotional well-being. All I wanted was to offer her some peace of mind and comfort, to be by her side as she navigated the storm of uncertainty that raged within her.

Despite my best efforts to reach out to her, Pari remained unreachable, her phone switched off and her whereabouts unknown. Desperate for any sign of reassurance, I turned to her roommate for answers, only to be met with the sobering reality that disturbing her in her vulnerable state would do more harm than good. With a heavy heart, I resigned myself to the agonising wait, grappling with feelings of helplessness and frustration as I pondered our next steps. Yet, even in the face of adversity, a glimmer of determination flickered to life within me, a resolve to overcome the challenges that lay ahead and emerge stronger for having weathered the storm together.

******

15. Pari's Plight

The next morning dawned with an eerie stillness that echoed devastating news swirling through the campus— Pari had taken her own life. The weight of shock and grief hung heavy in the air, casting a pall over the once vibrant atmosphere of our college community. It was as though the very essence of life had been sucked from the world, leaving us all adrift in a sea of sorrow and disbelief.

Unable to comprehend the enormity of what had transpired, I felt a surge of disbelief and desperation coursing through my veins. Without pausing to seek anyone's permission, I raced towards the hospital, each step a desperate plea for some shred of hope in the face of unspeakable tragedy. My mind raced with a thousand unanswered questions, each more agonising than the last. How could this have happened? What drove Pari to such desperate measures? And most hauntingly, was there anything I could have done to prevent it?

With each passing moment, the weight of dread grew heavier, threatening to suffocate me with its crushing presence. Yet, amidst the overwhelming despair, I clung to a flicker of hope that this news was somehow untrue, a cruel trick of fate that would be reversed with the dawn of a new day. Each heartbeat was a drumbeat of fear, each breath a prayer whispered into the void in the desperate hope of a miracle that would rewrite the tragic course of events.

Upon reaching the hospital, my heart pounded with desperate hope, clinging to the belief that somehow, someway, Pari would emerge unscathed from whatever ordeal had befallen her. However, my hopes were swiftly dashed as I was met by the sight of the proctor, engaged in a sombre conversation with police officials. Their grim expressions told a story of their own, confirming the heartbreaking reality that Pari was truly gone. The weight of their words hit me like a physical blow, leaving me reeling with disbelief and despair. Denied even the chance to see her one last time, I stood frozen in the sterile hospital corridor, grappling with the cruel finality of her absence.

Retreating to the hostel, I was enveloped in a suffocating blanket of sorrow and regret. Each step felt heavier than the last, as though the weight of Pari's loss was physically dragging me down. The vibrant light that was Pari, snuffed out by such cruel manipulation, left an emptiness that words could never hope to fill. Her absence echoed through the empty corridors of my mind, a constant reminder of the gaping void that now existed in my world. The pain of her loss was a searing ache that reverberated through every fibre of my being, a testament to the depth of the bond we had shared.

In the wake of Pari's untimely departure, I found myself grappling with the harsh realities of life's fragility and the devastating consequences of deception. Her loss served as a stark reminder of the fleeting nature of existence, a fragile thread that could be severed in an instant by the whims of fate. The pain of her absence was a poignant testament to the depth of the connection we had shared, a bond that transcended the confines of time and space. As I navigated the turbulent waters of grief, I clung to the memories of our time together, finding peace in the knowledge that Pari's spirit would forever live on in the hearts of those who loved her.

Pari's anguished face haunted my thoughts like a spectre, a constant presence that gnawed at the edges of my consciousness. Her sorrow, palpable and raw, seemed to seep into every crevice of my being, leaving me suffocating beneath the weight of guilt and remorse. It was as though her despair had become intertwined with my own, a tangled web of emotions that I couldn't unravel no matter how hard I tried.

With every passing moment, the burden of responsibility grew heavier, pressing down on me like a leaden weight. I couldn't shake the feeling that I had failed Pari, that my actions—or lack thereof—had played a pivotal role in her tragic fate. Her tear-streaked face haunted my dreams, her eyes filled with a silent plea for understanding and forgiveness that I couldn't bear to ignore. The knowledge that I had been powerless to shield her from the pain that ultimately consumed her left me wracked with anguish, a constant reminder of my own shortcomings and failings as a friend.

******

16. End of College Life

After Pari's death, I found myself engulfed by a profound sense of numbness. It felt as though the worst had already come to pass, leaving me adrift in a sea of sorrow. Every corner of the campus seemed to echo with her absence, a painful reminder of the loss that weighed heavily on my heart. I had no desire to linger in that place, to be reminded of all that had been lost. Despite my reluctance, I was ushered to the college counsellor's office, where I sat in silence, wrestling with the enormity of my grief. The minutes stretched into hours as I waited to be free from that confinement.

I still remember the date vividly—19th July. It was the first time my father set foot on the college campus. As he stood in the centre of the administrative office, surrounded by college authorities hurling accusations from all sides, his head hung as low as my conscience. The weight of shame and disappointment was almost tangible in the air. I wished desperately that I could change everything with a single flick, to erase the pain and humiliation that had descended upon us.

I tried to picture how I would confront him, rehearsing apologies and explanations in my mind, but my heart was heavy with dread. When I finally mustered the courage to approach, my father refused to see me. He sent a message instead, cold and final: there was no place for me at home anymore, and I was free to go wherever I wanted. The words hit me like a sledgehammer, leaving me reeling. My father, my rock, had disowned me, and the realisation shattered whatever was left of my spirit.

Within days, my world crumbled. I was friendless, college-less, hopeless, and now homeless. The once familiar campus that had been my second home now felt like a hostile territory. I wandered aimlessly, the weight of my belongings feeling heavier with each step. The faces that used to greet me with smiles and warmth now turned away in pity or disdain. I didn't know what to do, where to go, or whose help to seek. Desperation gripped me, and the future stretched out like a bleak, endless void.

I could clearly see glimpses of sympathy in the eyes of my warden, some of my classmates, and Raj. Yet, despite the concern etched on their faces, no one dared to come close or ask what I was going to do next. The unspoken pity was suffocating, a constant reminder of my isolation. Among the sea of indifferent faces, Shivam, the canteen Bhaiya, stood out. He was the only one who offered me a free meal and a place to stay in his small room outside the campus. His simple kindness brought tears to my eyes, a rare comfort amidst the overwhelming despair.

Raj, despite the fact that his earlier advice was denied by me, showed his true friendship during my darkest hour. He shared Johnson Sir's number with me, and, along with a few other classmates, managed to gather nearly Rs. 7000. Raj sent the money through Shivam Bhaiya, who handed it to me with a gentle pat on the back. When I met Johnson Sir at his institute—a charity organisation for underprivileged children—his compassionate eyes and warm smile offered a glimmer of hope. He listened to my story without judgement and extended his help, suggesting I go to one of his friends in Chennai who might offer me refuge and a fresh start.

Selling my phone, an expensive Samsung gifted by my father was one of the hardest decisions I've ever had to make. It was more than just a device; it was a symbol of happier times and my father's love. Parting with it felt like severing the last thread of connection to my past life. I managed to pocket Rs. 4200 for it, a paltry sum compared to its sentimental value. With a heavy heart, I left for Chennai, each mile taking me further away from my shattered world but also towards a faint, uncertain promise of a new beginning. The journey was filled with a mixture of fear, sorrow, and fragile hope, as I clung to the belief that somehow, I would find my way through the darkness.

******

17. Chennai Episode

In my darkest hour, it was Johnson Sir who emerged as a guiding light, offering not just practical assistance but also a comforting presence that eased the weight of my sorrow. He took charge of arranging my journey back to Chennai, booking my ticket and providing me with one thousand rupees despite my initial reluctance. His insistence on helping me, coupled with his genuine concern, touched me deeply, reminding me that even in times of despair, there are still those who care.

But Johnson Sir's kindness didn't end there. He went above and beyond to ensure my well-being, sharing the address and contact details of the person I needed to meet upon my arrival in Chennai. With his comforting words and reassuring presence, he saw me off at the station, his gestures of kindness offering relief in the midst of my grief. As I boarded the train, a sense of gratitude washed over me, knowing that I had someone like Johnson Sir looking out for me in my time of need. His compassion and support were a beacon of hope in the darkness, guiding me through the storm with unwavering warmth and generosity.

When I was about to reach Chennai, panic set in as I tried to look for my diary where I had written the address and contact details of the person I was supposed to meet. To my ill luck, I discovered that I had lost the diary somewhere along the way. This realisation added to my misery, making life in Chennai even tougher than I had expected.

With no address or contact details, I found myself marred by hunger, despair, and helplessness. As a Hindi-speaking boy, navigating the bustling and unfamiliar surroundings of Chennai Central Railway Station became an overwhelming ordeal. I wandered for hours, lugging my bucket, mug, a big trolley bag, and a quilt, desperately trying to figure out where to go. Just when hope seemed to be slipping away, an auto-driver, a kind-hearted Sardar Ji, agreed to give me a ride and helped me.

Sardar Ji introduced me to a man who offered me lodging and a job at a canteen near Ganesha Institute. The room was small and bare, but it was a sanctuary compared to the hot and humid streets. The job at the canteen was gruelling, but it kept me occupied and gave me a small income. Each day was a struggle, marred by long hours and physical exhaustion, yet I found a sliver of solace in the routine. I was grateful to Sardar Ji for facilitating this lifeline and to the canteen owner for his kindness, which provided a semblance of stability amidst the chaos.

For days, I couldn't sleep. The memories of my expulsion from college, Pari's tragic end, and Krishav's cruel betrayal haunted me relentlessly. The weight of these events pressed down on me, making it nearly impossible to find any peace. The nights were the worst, filled with sleepless hours and racing thoughts that left me feeling utterly exhausted. I missed my mother and my family deeply, but the pain of being disowned made reaching out to them seem pointless.

In my isolation, I found a small lifeline through Orkut. Desperate for some connection to my past, I managed to contact my brother. Seeing his name pop up on my screen brought a rush of bittersweet emotions—relief mingled with the ache of separation. Through Orkut, I also reconnected with some of my college friends like Rahul Tripathi. Each connection was a thread that tied me back to a life that felt increasingly distant.

These online interactions became my respite. Conversations with my brother and old friends provided a temporary escape from my harsh reality. They reminded me that there were still people who cared about me, even if they were miles away. Yet, the virtual support could only do so much. The memories and the pain remained, and each day was a struggle to keep moving forward. But these connections gave me a glimmer of hope, a faint reminder that I wasn't completely alone in the world.

This struggle continued for more than five months. My situation gradually improved, but the language barrier and cultural differences made life in Chennai isolating. My time in Chennai, working at the Canteen of Ganesha helped me enhance my communication skills and I started communicating in English, although not fluently.

As the suggestion of relocating to Delhi lingered in the air, offered by both a regular customer and echoed by the canteen owner, it sparked a flicker of hope within me. Their words, tinged with the promise of belonging and opportunity, stirred a mix of emotions—hope, trepidation, and a whisper of possibility. Despite the uncertainty that loomed over another move, I couldn't ignore the tantalising prospect of finding a community where I might finally feel at home.

With each step toward this new chapter, I carried with me the weight of previous beginnings and the resilience forged through each transition. The decision to uproot once more was daunting, yet my resolve remained unshaken. I was determined to embrace the unknown, to seek out a place where I could not only survive but thrive. It was a leap of faith, propelled by the belief that amidst the unfamiliarity of a new city, I could carve out a space to rebuild, grow, and discover a sense of belonging that had eluded me thus far.

So, with hope as my compass and determination as my guide, I embarked on the journey to Delhi—a journey marked by uncertainty but buoyed by the unwavering belief that with each step forward, I moved closer to a place I could finally call home.

.

****

18. Delhi Episode

I started for Delhi with a new hope and vigour. The train was packed with people, and I somehow managed to board the second class with all my belongings. Within 10 minutes of the train's departure, the ticket checker approached and imposed a fine of 3000 rupees on me. I tried to explain my situation in broken English, but he was unyielding. The anxiety of my journey compounded by this sudden financial burden left me feeling utterly hopeless.

HIGHS LOWS

At that moment, a kind man named Mr. Rao happened to pass by. He noticed my desperate attempts to explain myself to the ticket checker and, without hesitation, paid the fine on my behalf. I was overwhelmed with gratitude and disbelief at this unexpected kindness. Mr Reddy then invited me to sit near his berth, and as the train chugged along towards Delhi, I poured out my entire story to him—my expulsion, Pari's tragic end, and the betrayal by Krishav.

Listening intently, Mr. Rao sympathised deeply with my plight. He offered not just words of comfort, but a lifeline. As the director of a reputed institute in Delhi, he extended a job offer to help me get back on my feet. His generosity was a beacon of hope in my darkest hours. The journey to Delhi, which began with fear and uncertainty, now seemed to hold a promise of a new beginning. Mr Reddy's unexpected kindness rekindled my faith in humanity and gave me the strength to face whatever lay ahead.

My journey in Delhi began humbly, as an office boy earning a modest salary of 4000 rupees per month. Despite my lowly position, I found myself gravitating towards Mr Rao's cabin and Kiran Ma'am's reception desk, drawn by their warmth and encouragement. Mr. Rao took me under his wing, encouraging me to converse with him in English and patiently correcting my mistakes along the way. His unwavering support and belief in my potential gradually became a beacon of inspiration for me, spurring me to strive for excellence despite my humble beginnings.

At times, Kiran Ma'am would kindly allow me to interact with the parents and customers, giving me the opportunity to practise speaking in English. I relished these moments, feeling a surge of confidence with each conversation. It was empowering to communicate effectively in a language that had once felt daunting, and I found myself growing more self-assured with each interaction. Their encouragement and belief in my abilities bolstered my confidence, reminding me that with determination and perseverance, I could overcome any obstacle that came my way.

One day, Mr. Rao approached me with an unexpected proposition that left me utterly stunned. He had noticed my dedication and progress, and he asked me if I had ever considered teaching. The mere suggestion seemed surreal to me. As a simple 12th-pass student with no formal degree or teaching experience, the idea of becoming an educator in such a prestigious institution felt like a far-fetched dream. I couldn't help but question whether Mr. Rao was joking, but his sincerity was unmistakable. In a single moment, he shattered the limitations I had placed on myself and opened up a world of possibilities I had never dared to imagine. On that pivotal day, Mr Rao took a monumental step by enrolling me on a degree course at the School of Open Learning (SOL), Delhi. It was a gesture of unwavering faith and belief in my potential, one that would forever alter the trajectory of my life. With Mr. Rao's guidance and encouragement, I embarked on a journey as a teacher—a journey filled with challenges and triumphs, but one that I embraced wholeheartedly. His unwavering support served as a beacon of hope, propelling me forward even when doubts threatened to hold me back. I am eternally grateful for his belief in me, for it was his encouragement that ignited the flame of possibility within me and set me on a path towards realising my dreams.

I was presented with a unique opportunity to teach the aspirants of LDCE (Limited Departmental Competitive Examination), a significant exam tailored for central government employees. The opportunity to teach aspirants of the LDCE was unlike anything I had ever imagined and I felt a deep sense of responsibility in guiding these candidates towards success. Despite the unconventional timing of the classes—often scheduled late at night or in the early hours of the morning—I welcomed the challenge with open arms. While finding a permanent teacher willing to accommodate such irregular hours proved to be difficult, for me, it was a blessing in disguise. With Mr. Rao's steadfast support, I embraced this opportunity as a chance to showcase my dedication and passion for teaching. Under Mr Rao's guidance, I dove headfirst into this new endeavour, determined to make the most of every moment. He entrusted me with the responsibility of teaching these candidates, assuring me that I could dedicate my days to studying and preparing for the classes scheduled at odd times. His belief in my abilities fuelled my determination, motivating me to go above and beyond to ensure the success of my students.

With access to reference books and the internet at my disposal, I delved deep into the subject matter, driven by a burning desire to share knowledge and empower others on their journey to success. As I embarked on teaching these classes, I encountered some initial apprehension from the learners. Many of these aspirants were young adults, some much older and more experienced than I was. However, with Sir's invaluable guidance and my relentless efforts, I gradually managed to alleviate their concerns and instil confidence through my teaching.

*****

19. The Turning Point

On 19th January 2009, the miracle did happen with Mr. Iyangar, a man of strong build in his late 30s, an aspirant of LDCE, successfully qualified the exam, attributing his success to my guidance. As I witnessed the joy radiating from his countenance, a kaleidoscope of emotions swirled within me, blending awe with humility and pride with a tinge of disbelief. Was it truly my guidance that propelled him to this pinnacle of success, or was it the convergence of fate and unwavering determination?

In that moment of profound gratitude, as I knelt before Mr. Rao, the architect of countless dreams transformed into reality, tears cascaded down like a river unleashed. Each drop bore witness to the countless nights of toil, the relentless pursuit of excellence, and the unwavering belief in the power of mentorship. With trembling lips and a heart overflowing with emotion, I conveyed my deepest appreciation, knowing that his unwavering support had been the anchor amidst life's tempestuous seas. For in that juncture where destiny intertwined with human endeavour, it was not just Mr Iyangar's victory that reverberated through the chambers of my soul; it was the affirmation of the profound impact of guidance and mentorship in shaping destinies and lighting the way amidst the darkness.

In the bustling world of coaching institutes, where accolades often accompany pedigrees and credentials wield immense power, my ascent was nothing short of extraordinary. A product of the Hindi medium education system, devoid of formal accolades, I defied conventional norms with my mastery of English grammar and a penchant for yielding exceptional results in competitive examinations such as NDA, CDS, SSC, and LDCE. In the labyrinthine streets of the suburbs, my name resonated like a whispered hymn of triumph, spoken with reverence among both aspirants and seasoned mentors.

Amidst this recognition, Mr Rao emerged as a beacon of support and staunch belief in my potential. His actions spoke volumes, extending beyond mere words of encouragement. Through his efforts, he orchestrated a pivotal moment in my journey, arranging accommodation for me alongside Mr. Sethi, an illustrious alumnus of IIT-Chennai and a revered figure in the realm of Mathematics education. Sharing a room with such a luminary felt akin to stepping into the hallowed pages of legend, where wisdom and brilliance intertwined seamlessly. It was a dreamlike moment, where the boundaries between aspiration and reality blurred, and the echoes of possibility reverberated through the corridors of my soul. Amidst the anticipation of meeting Mr. Sethi, I found myself weaving through countless tales of his brilliance, painting mental portraits of an intellectual giant. Yet, when the moment of encounter arrived, I was met not with airs of grandeur, but with the warmth of simplicity. Mr. Sethi, with his unassuming demeanour and approachable aura, shattered the pedestal I had unwittingly placed him upon. It was a humbling realisation – that greatness need not wear the armour of arrogance. In that shared space, anecdotes flowed freely, punctuated by hilarity and healthy chatting, bridging the chasm between admiration and familiarity. Indeed, meeting Mr. Sethi was a lesson not only in academic prowess but also in the richness of humility, leaving an indelible mark on my journey of learning and growth. Meeting Mr. Sethi was not just a rendezvous with a renowned scholar; it was an invitation to embrace the richness of humility and the beauty of authentic connection. His presence left an indelible mark on my journey of learning and growth, a reminder that true greatness lies not in the grandiose, but in the simple act of being oneself.

******

20. Realisation, Regret, and Gratitude

"How did you reunite with your family?" Richa, who had been listening to me intently, interrupted with a question that tugged at my heartstrings.

The journey to reconnect with my family unfolded as a blend of technological marvel and emotional turbulence, each step marked by the delicate dance between hope and hesitation. With the aid of the internet, particularly through my connection with my brother on Orkut, I took a tentative stride towards bridging the chasm that had separated us for so long. Updating my profile with my new contact information and the announcement of my relocation to Delhi felt like a small yet significant gesture—a flicker of hope amidst the vast expanse of uncertainty.

As my brother reached out, his curiosity and concern palpable through the digital ether, I found myself grappling with conflicting emotions. His inquiries about my plans in Delhi stirred a plethora of thoughts and emotions, each one vying for dominance within the confines of my heart. Yet, when pressed about my intentions, I spoke of my newfound position at a prestigious coaching institute, a glimmer of pride mingled with defiance in my voice.

The day the call came, summoning me back home after 15 long months of relentless struggle, was a seismic moment in my life—a tidal wave of emotions crashing over me with unparalleled intensity. The mere prospect of reuniting with my mother, after what felt like an eternity of separation, ignited an uncanny sense of joy and relief within the depths of my soul.

Yet, amidst the euphoria that threatened to engulf me, there lingered an unexpected intruder—a stubborn sense of pride, seasoned by the unexpected turn of events that had led me to secure a position of prominence. In the crucible of my ego, forged by the trials of adversity, I found myself standing firm, resolute in my decision to chart my own course, regardless of the beckoning call of home.

With a stern resolve, I bluntly denied the plea to return, the weight of my newfound position lending an air of defiance to my words. In that moment of steadfast refusal, I allowed the tendrils of ego to entwine themselves around my heart, obscuring the bittersweet ache of longing that pulsed beneath the surface.

Little did I realise, in my fervent determination to carve out a path of my own, that the true measure of strength lay not in the armour of pride, but in the vulnerability of humility and the courage to embrace the ties that bind us to those we hold dear.

HIGHS LOWS

I was under the illusion that the reputation of the institute seemed to have softened my father's anger. It was as if the name of the institute had the power to validate my struggles and aspirations. That's why, despite the fervent entreaties of my family, each call from my mother a poignant reminder of the ties that bound us, I remained resolute in my decision. Whether fuelled by ego, fear, or a potent cocktail of both, I couldn't bring myself to yield to their pleas. In that moment of stubborn resolve, I chose to forge ahead, guided by the belief that my path lay not in retracing my steps, but in carving out a new destiny amidst the bustling streets of Delhi.

The burden of regret weighed heavily on my heart, a heavy cloak woven from the threads of missed opportunities and misplaced pride. Looking back on my decision to stay away from home, driven by ego and ambition, I'm haunted by the nagging thought of what might have been. Despite the forgiving embrace of my parents, my stubbornness overshadowed their love, leaving me adrift in a sea of remorse.

The news of my father's silent battle with cancer struck me like a thunderbolt, shattering the illusion of distance that had kept me estranged from my family. For three agonising months, his suffering remained a closely guarded secret, hidden beneath the facade of everyday life. How could I have been so blind, so consumed by my own ambitions, that I failed to notice the silent cries of a father in need?

Alone in my room, tears flowed freely, each drop a painful reminder of the gulf that had widened between us. The walls of pride crumbled in the face of overwhelming grief, leaving me exposed and vulnerable to the harsh reality of my own mistakes. In that moment of reckoning, I found myself grappling with the bitter consequences of my own folly, yearning for a chance to turn back the hands of time and make amends before it was too late.

That very evening, without waiting for any call, or anything I left for my place. Stepping into my home, I was met with tears, hugs, and an unspoken understanding that we had all been through our own battles. My mother's embrace, warm and forgiving, melted away the months of pain and separation. It wasn't just a reunion; it was a renewal of bonds, a reminder that no matter how far we wander, the love of family remains a constant, unwavering force.

Stepping into my father's room felt like traversing a minefield of emotions, each step heavier than the last as I braced myself for the inevitable confrontation. In his tear-stained eyes, I glimpsed an ocean of anger, helplessness, and beneath it all, a flicker of unyielding love. Oh, how I longed to turn back the hands of time, to rewrite the script of my past mistakes.

As the months went by, my father's health continued to be delicate, stretched thin by the unrelenting grip of cancer. But in the face of it all, despite all that he was going through, there was something in his eyes that refused to be extinguished. Despite the agony, there was a glimmer of hope that no chemotherapy or radiation could douse. It wasn't just a defiance against the disease; it was a defiance against the years of tension that had pulled us apart. He wasn't ready to let go—not of life, not of family, not of me.

One late evening, just when I thought the weight of regret had completely overwhelmed me, I saw him. My father, frail but resolute, sitting at the kitchen table, trying to get a spoonful of soup into his mouth. It struck me how much he had aged, how much he had suffered in silence. I stood in the doorway, unable to move, the magnitude of my own selfishness crashing over me. My heart clenched with guilt, but the love I saw in his eyes melted the ice that had encased my pride for so long.

"Ravi," he whispered, his voice weak, but full of warmth.

I stepped forward, every part of me trembling. "I'm sorry, Baba... I should have been here. I should have seen you... been there for you."

Tears welled up in his eyes. But instead of the anger I had braced myself for, I saw only compassion. "You don't have to apologize, *beta*. You did what you had to. I understand. I was wrong to let my pride build walls between us. We all make mistakes."

I knelt beside him, overwhelmed by the depth of his forgiveness. In that moment, I realized that our bond was unbreakable, despite the years of distance, despite the mistakes.

The next few weeks were a blur of hospital visits, anxiety, and sleepless nights. But something remarkable happened. My father, who had been so frail, began to fight back. It was as if his own stubborn will to survive, to be there for his family, found new strength in the face of love. With each passing day, his condition improved just a little bit more. We celebrated small victories: a breath without pain, a night without the persistent cough, a meal he could keep down. And through it all, the bond between us, once shattered by pride, grew stronger and I spent every possible moment by his side, holding his hand, reminding him that he wasn't alone. In return, he shared stories of his youth, of his struggles, of the dreams he once had. For the first time in years, we talked not just as father and son, but as two men, connected by shared experiences, understanding each other in ways we never had before. It was during one of those quiet moments, sitting in the hospital room with my father and my mother at my side, that I realized the real meaning of family. It wasn't about pride or accomplishments or the things I had thought would define me. It was about love—the quiet, unwavering love that always endures. Family wasn't something I could escape; it was the very foundation of who I was, and no amount of distance or ambition could change that.

The day the doctors finally told us that the treatment had worked, that my father was in remission, was a day I would never forget. My father's eyes, tired but alight with a spark of victory, met mine. And in that moment, I knew we had both fought our battles—his against cancer, and mine against my own pride—and we had won. Together. We returned home, not just to a house, but to a new beginning. My family, now healed in both body and spirit, embraced me with the understanding that had once seemed so elusive. No longer was I defined by my mistakes or my ambition. I was defined by the love that had carried me through, the love that had brought me home.

As I looked around, at my father sitting strong in his favourite chair, my mother's radiant smile, I felt a deep, unshakable peace settle within me. There were still challenges ahead, of course. Life would always be full of highs and lows. And in that moment, I knew that home, whether it was a place or a person, was where the true power to heal and transform our lives lay. The journey I had taken to rebuild my life, from the depths of despair to this moment of joy, had brought me full circle. I was no longer just Ravi, the boy who had been lost and broken. I was Ravi, someone who had learned that in the end, love and family are what make us whole.

That was the greatest victory of all.

*****

HIGHS LOWS

www.ingramcontent.com/pod-product-compliance
Lightning Source LLC
LaVergne TN
LVHW041615070526
838199LV00052B/3159